W9-AZG-291

The End of Peril, the End of Enmity, the End of Strife, a Haven

The End of Peril,
the End of Enmity,
the End of Strife,
a Haven

Thirii Myo Kyaw Myint

Copyright © 2018 by Thirii Myo Kyaw Myint
ISBN 978-1-934819-74-6

Cover and Book Design by Steve Halle

Published By Noemi Press, Inc. A Nonprofit Literary Organization.
www.noemipress.org

for my mother

The End of Peril, the End of Enmity, the End of Strife, a Haven

THE WOODS ARE GONE NOW. A quiet lingers where they used to be, as if a weight had been held there, between the trees. Even with the trees gone, the weight remains. There is no sound.

MY MOTHER TOLD ME OF the woods; they grew thick and sweet at the back of the house when she was a girl. Only a chain link fence stands there now. Behind the fence is an empty lot where once there was a building under construction. The air moves differently on the other side of the fence. I can see a slight refraction, a bending of light, a rustling of leaves that hang from phantom branches.

It is like a place where people have died.

Where my mother died, I think, for I feel her body is buried there in the ground, at the foot of the trees that no longer grow. My mother is not dead, but it is as if she has already died. As if this city has killed her. When I look at my mother, her body is too light. The weight of her body lies in the ground. I will mark her grave with a pile of stones, carefully stacked. The air moves. The stones hold. The fence moves. It is a rat, I think, a creature with claws and teeth and hungry. The animals in this city are misshapen. I do not know what exactly animals should look like, but I know these ones are wrong.

◆ ◆ ◆

She showed her palm to me once when we were younger.

See this line? my mother said, tracing an arc at the base of her thumb.

It's the life line, she said. Mine curves back, so I will die in the place where I was born.

I wanted my mother to live forever. I begged her never to go back to that place.

In this harbor city, the streets are unpaved and my feet soon cake with mud. The dogs in the street are red-eyed and vicious, shackled to shops on short metal chains or galloping mad in packs. Children run naked from the waist down and fight off the dogs.

I am afraid for the baby in my care. The baby I carried out of the dome and across the ocean to this city. If I leave the baby in the street, the dogs will devour it. Maybe the children too. I have not yet chosen a name for the baby. I have not yet chosen a gender. There is so much to choose, to give, and by giving, to take away. I do not want to take away from the baby. It is the second precept, to refrain from taking what is not freely given. The baby was freely given to me.

I turn the corner and the street widens. Food cart men pedal past, ringing their sad, sweet bells. The baby enjoys the bells. It squirms in my arms. In the street are young girls stooped under the weight of their wares, balanced across the shoulders on long poles. Some of the girls carry babies strapped to their backs. At the end of the street, I reach the railroad crossing. Old men sit by the tracks and chew betel nut and spit red. They sit there, on rain buckets or three-pronged stools, and they look at me. I hold the baby closer. I feel ashamed.

They named this city the end of peril, the men who fought in the king's war. There were many kings in the history of this country. There were many wars.

The king's men retreated here when they could no longer hold back the enemy. The end of peril, they called the city. The end of enmity. The end of strife. It meant all of those things. The city was their haven. It was an afterlife for those who had not yet died.

And though I have not yet died, though I have lived, through the breach of the dome and its evacuation, this harbor city is not my haven.

In the domed city of my girlhood, the city from which I escaped with the baby, I lived in a house with my mother and father. We lived on a tree-lined street with painted mailboxes and verdant front lawns. My father inherited our house from his father, who had been the architect of the dome. My father was always ill. My mother kept me home from school because she needed help caring for him. My mother was lonely. I was allowed to play outside only when she took her siesta.

I liked to play in the woods at the end of our street. The woods my father's father had transplanted from the end of peril. They sprawled all along the edges of the dome, to create the illusion that there was no dome, no wall enclosing the city. The woods thickened just a mile from the street, and the dirt paths dissolved into undergrowth. That is where I met the girl.

The day I found her in the woods, the girl was running away. She had a backpack full of snacks and underwear. I saw the backpack first, before I saw her. It was baby blue, scratched up with ink. I nudged it with my foot and a sandwich spilled from the broken zipper. When I looked up the girl was standing just a few feet away, in a pair of white underpants, arms crossed over her naked chest.

Hi, I said.

What are you doing here? she said.

I live here, I pointed in the direction of the street.

The girl dropped her arms and placed her hands on her hips. Her chest was as flat as mine.

I haven't seen you at school, the girl said.

I shook my head.

I don't go.

Why not?

I shrugged.

The girl gave me a look over.

Okay, she said. So do you want to play?

Yes.

I wanted to very much.

THE ANIMALS IN THIS HARBOR CITY have too many eyes or limbs growing in the wrong places. They move too quietly for their numbers.

Most days I do not leave the house. I travelled a great distance to return to this city, this city where I was born, and I am fatigued by the journey. It is a relief to be still, to listen to animals scurry through the walls or under the teak floor boards. It is cool inside the house, and there are many books in my grandfather's study. Most are written in languages I cannot read. I do not mind. I like to smell the books. I like to turn the pages and feel the paper, thin and smooth, between my fingers.

My grandfather does not speak to me.

He thinks I am an imbecile.

Mostly he sleeps in the arm chair with his cane leaned against the table. He snores. His snoring wakes the baby. The baby's crying wakes my grandfather. He always pretends he had not been sleeping. He wipes the rheum from his eyes with a handkerchief, adjusts his spectacles, and carries on with the book in his lap.

I spend my days in the study because there are no windows there. It is as if the city outside were any other place.

My mother does not let me forget I am descended also from the enemy. The raiders from the north who drove the king's men to the end of peril.

You are a nomad, my mother always said. Restless, a hungry ghost.

My father's mother was the daughter of a clan leader, an heiress to conquered land, a descendent of the northern invaders. She carried the enemy bloodline into my body. From her, I inherited a body built for violence. Built to endure violence, but also to commit it.

You are always in search of that fertile valley, my mother said.

This harbor city is not it. I am an invader here.

In this city, the sky is retreating from the earth. Every day it looks fainter and farther away. I think of a story I had read as a girl, of women in a village who carved up the sky for food until the sky flew away in anger. In fear, I always thought, not anger, for hungry women must be frightening.

I stand by the chain link fence at the back of my grandfather's house and tell this story to the baby. I want it to better understand what it is like to be a woman, for the baby may one day become a woman. I grip the baby firmly under its armpits and raise it above my head and I say to the baby, Take a bite of the sky, go ahead. And the baby gurgles and I move my arms up and down and it squeals and I say, Baby, did you know once there were trees? And I tell the baby about the trees in the domed city, the woods where the girl and I had played together as children. I tell the baby about the textures of bark, the shapes of fruit, the smell of white-petaled flowers. I try to describe the sound of wind rustling through leaves, the way the leaves would flutter, and how the sunlight was tinged green inside the woods, how clear that light was. I explain to the baby that the trees were given names, but the names didn't matter because the trees didn't know about them and maybe wouldn't have liked them.

I hold the baby close to me again, and I say very softly that the women were blamed for the sky flying away, because women are usually blamed, and I can't explain this to the baby, but I look at its soft, round face for a while and I try to make it understand. The choice of gender the baby will one day make is heavy. Choice or discovery, I say to the baby, though discoveries are made also. Everything to make, to create, to do. The baby feels so heavy in my arms. As heavy as a hundred years, one stone for each year, the stones piled carefully over the grave.

The baby must not die. I think this even as I look upon my mother's grave. The one I imagined for her in the empty lot at the back of the house, in the ground dusted with concrete. The baby must live. It was born in the domed city, and now that the dome has collapsed, I am the one who must keep it safe. The baby lived through the breach, and it must live through the renewal that will follow. The replenishing of the forests and the lakes and the rivers. The baby is a part of the renewal, I think, for it grows as the trees are still growing in the domed city, or what is left of it. I believe the baby and the trees will grow until they are reunited here, at the end of peril. I believe the baby will bring the renewal to this city.

The baby must live. I knew this even before the baby was born. My mother had taught me about reproduction when I was a girl, and I never understood that word, for nothing is created again, but always created for the first time.

They were brutes, the king's enemy, beastly. Their only religion was the worship of those among them who had died green deaths, untimely deaths, deaths at the hands of tyrannical kings. A mountain was sacred to them, an ancient volcano, for the blood of the ones who were killed there mixed with ash and turned almost green. The enemy painted their faces with this blood-green ash and to the king's people they looked like ogres, the man-eating kind, with long, straight fangs.

The king was afraid. He lost the war. People were killed on both sides, animals drowned, fishing villages were sacked, the fields left to rot, and the river set on fire. The city fell and the two peoples are one people now.

In my body, I am one person.

My father's father built the domed city. He is called the city's architect. He built the red-bricked streets, and the white-shuttered houses, and the artificial lake in the city center, the school and the hospital on the banks of the lake. He built the opera house, and the museum, and the domed sky, where the moon and the stars were projected each night. He built the vertical farms and the rooftop gardens and the outdoor market that stayed open year-round. He built everything in the dome, but he never had a chance to live there himself. He died soon after I was born. Genetic disease, the same one that would strike my father.

Before he died, my father's father uprooted all the trees from the end of peril and transplanted them in the dome. This is how my father tells the story, though I know that no ship nor plane could carry a forest of trees across the ocean. I know that my father's father studied botany and learned how to grow trees from seeds. I know that he studied biochemistry and learned how to grow them in years, rather than decades or centuries. Still, I like the way my father tells the story. I like to imagine the trees uprooted and replanted one by one. The tedium of that, the futility.

THE MIRRORS IN THIS HOUSE are covered with cloth, and I do not bother to unveil them. The cloth protects the mirrors from dust and the spirits of the dead.

Ghosts live in mirrors, my mother always said.

I find my mother in her old room, the one she had slept in as a child. She is sitting at the dressing table, gazing into the oval mirror that leans against the wall. She asks me to take her picture. She has a camera ready.

She has made herself up in my grandmother's jewelry, diamonds and rubies, sapphires and pearls. They dangle in teardrops from her ears, neck, and wrists. A heavy ring adorns each finger. Her bangs are curled so you cannot see that she is balding. The part in her hair widening at the top of her head, like a river widening as it flows into the sea. My mother's beauty has emptied as well.

But not into me, the way it should have, from mother to daughter.

I take her picture by the dressing table. She directs me to angle the camera so you can see her reflection in the mirror, but not mine. This is the same pose she held on her wedding day. This is the same oval mirror. I peer through the lens, and I do not know how my mother will bear it, to see this photograph alongside the old one.

My mother says I brought her back to this city.

She says my life line cuts the palm in two. My line runs straight, like a knife.

If you stay in this place, my mother says to me, this place where you were born, you will live forever.

My father died in this city. That is what I will tell the baby someday. I will say he walked to the river and drowned, and when they found his body, several weeks later, he had been devoured so thoroughly by fish they could hardly identify him as my father.

I feel they will never identify him, this man who died in the river. That way, he will and will not definitively be my father. He will be mine, without the burden of fact. The fact is, there is no man in the river. There is no suicide, and my father is probably still alive.

He is an invalid. That kind of man does not die.

I left him in the domed city far from here, in the house where he had lived with me and my mother, on a tree-lined street, the trees multiplying even on that first day of the breach, the woods at the end of the street glutted, already rising in a wall of green.

Our house stood at the edge of the city, at the base of the cresting trees, and I left my father there.

I left the domed city with only the clothes on my body and the baby in my arms. The baby is swaddled to my chest now as I walk to the river. It is a long walk from my grandfather's house, a day-long excursion, through narrow, crowded streets and across shadeless paddy fields, but there was no moving water in the domed city, and I want to see what a river looks like. When I was young my father told me stories about a burning river where a war was fought between two peoples. The river in his stories is the same river I am walking to now. It was a watery grave for those who died in that ancient war, and my mother says even today the inhabitants of this city scatter the ashes of their dead in the river.

When the baby and I finally reach the water, women are fishing along the bank and their children and catches bake together in the sun. The children are bloated with shriveled limbs and the fish look reptilian, all scales and meat. The river is brown and grey, reflecting the colors of the sky. The water moves languidly, thickly, like a tongue. It would be easy to drown in such a river, I think, for my father or anyone. I have outfitted the baby with a filter mask, but still, it begins to cry. The river smells of sewage and burnt plastic.

The enemy came from a land of ice where all was dead and ash. The enemy could speak to the dead, and the dead told them secrets. The green dead, the un-ripened dead. They led the enemy down from the sacred volcano, from their mass grave, across mountains of ice, through blue snow and blistering wind, with the promise of a fertile valley.

After several months, the enemy descended the foothills in the north. Weary, and dizzy from the surfeit of oxygen, they rested in the valley there. Many had died on the journey through the mountains: men, women, children, and beasts. The ones who lived did not rest for long. The land in the north was unyielding. Crops which had thrived on lush volcanic slopes did not bear fruit in the rocky valley.

Then the hot season came and the sun rose redder every day. Streams dried and a drought wrung out the land. The enemy could not bear the heat. Mirages burned their eyes. They lost more of their numbers.

In the north, the river flowed underground, invisible, and the enemy followed it south by instinct. In the same way, they killed.

In the domed city, the runaway girl was my closest friend. She made my mother jealous. My mother's mother had been a harpist and my mother's body was formed in the same way. It was a body made to kneel. The girl had the same body, childlike and pliable. Her wrists were so small I could circle them between my thumb and pinky finger. My wrists were thick and my body solid. The girl looked more like my mother's daughter than I did.

And the girl could have been my mother's daughter because her own mother was dead. The girl lived with her grandmother. The girl said her mother was dead but her mother was in a submarine at the bottom of the sea. To the girl, the war raging outside the dome was death. The girl spoke often of her father. She spoke of him in the present tense, what he liked or disliked, the things he said. It was only through my mother that I learned that the girl's father was the one who was really dead.

I was allowed to play in the woods with the girl only one hour a day. My mother educated me at home, and my education was accelerated. School dulled the brain, my mother said. The children there did not learn algebra until they were fourteen. By then, my mother said, I would be studying calculus, organic chemistry, and history up to last dynasty.

The girl hated school, but she hated my mother more. She felt sorry for me. Every day, at the hour when my mother took her siesta, the girl would meet me outside our house, and we would race to the woods at the end of the street. The woods were green in the domed city, and the animals so perfect. The girl and I named the trees and the shrubs, we gathered flowers and searched for bugs. Sometimes we would squat on our haunches in our underwear and dig out rocks with our bare hands. We removed our clothes to avoid getting mud on them, or sweat, or blood. To avoid punishment when we went home for dinner.

We also liked to be naked. We felt like young animals.

The rocks we dug were round and smooth and identical and I knew my father's father had placed them there in the ground, but I played along with the girl. She said the rocks were ancient, from a time before time was measured. She said the rocks knew stories of the primordial sea, the first life forms, the continents of ice and the eruptions of ash that blackened the sky. We lay on our backs in the cool mud of the earth, which my father's father had also manufactured, and told these stories to each other, feeling the mud dry gently on our bodies, looking up at the trees and the blue-domed sky.

My mother says this harbor city is decapitated. What she means is, the trees are gone. Not just the ones at the back of my grandfather's house, but all the trees in the city. Even the street lamps have fallen in the last storm.

Though I have not been in this city long enough to see its sallow moon grow full, I have already observed a number of storms. It rains here almost every day. My mother says this is because I returned in the rainy season. My mother is not afraid of the storms; she watches them with pleasure from her window, though they seem to grow in intensity each time they arrive.

The people of this city also welcome the rains. My grandfather says the rainwater is full of toxic chemicals, but I have seen children bathing in it and singing. I have seen families collect the rainwater in plastic buckets to use for their washing and cooking. I have seen the street dogs fornicate in the midst of a storm. The rainy season is a time of rest and rejuvenation, my mother says, when the dry earth is replenished for the rice planting to begin. I hope the rains will also replenish the earth for the trees to grow again, for the renewal to come to this city.

It never rained in the domed city of my girlhood. The woods were misted, like the crops in the warehouses, but the domed sky remained blue. The sound of rain is unfamiliar to me. Its incessant pounding. The rain seems to come from all directions. I do not believe that it falls from the sky. In this harbor city, so close to the ocean and yet protected from it on three sides, the rain is the ocean's claim on the city. The storms are the ocean's revenge.

The baby has been coughing since our walk to the river, so I have given it some syrup. I will not leave the house again until the baby is better. I sit in the nursery while it sleeps and I watch the rain. The window in the nursery faces the ocean and the rain hits the glass directly. If I open the window, the rain would drench my face and my hair; I believe it would drown me.

The enemy chief was a ruthless man, they said, the king's people. He was a great warrior. He devoured the hearts of those he had defeated because he believed it gave him strength. And it is true I am descended also from the enemy for inside my chest beat various hearts and I am strong. I was strong enough to carry my father out of the domed city, though I did not do it. The enemy chief had carried his mother and father on each broad shoulder down from the mountains of ice. He had led his people from their sacred volcano to the rock valley in the north; he had led them along the underground river, south to the sea. He had chopped off the tongues, hands, and feet of those who would rival or desert him. He had chopped off their heads.

The chief had a son, an only child like myself, and the boy was to be the next chief. Only the boy did not want to be chief.

He was afraid to kill. When the heat of the sun bore down at midday, the boy would sit under the shade of a fruit-bearing tree and think of the icy land from which his people came. He would think of the sacred mountain where his mother died, the chieftess of the clan. She had died at the hands of a tyrannical king; she had died a martyr.

The chief's son was not afraid to die as he was afraid to kill. He only wanted to die well. He wanted to die courageously.

For many years in the domed city, I helped my mother care for my father until it was my mother who was helping me and then no one. One day my mother said my education was complete and the next day she left the city. She left years before the breach, and yet her leaving was the first day of the breach, for before she left I had not believed the dome was permeable.

My mother said there was nothing more she could teach me. She said it was a shame I wasn't beautiful. She left me a document that would grant me passage to follow her, if my father died. Where I am going, my mother said, everything is dead. But they say it will come back to life. The living will choke on their excess of life and the dead will breathe.

In this city we have returned to, my mother is choking. She returned too soon. The average man lives twenty-five years in this country and the average woman thirty-five. My mother has grown old in her child's body. The people of this city wait for the renewal to arrive, for the trees to grow again, but my mother cannot wait much longer.

◆ ◆ ◆

When my father's father was a young man, he watched all the trees in his native country die. He watched the rivers dry and the lakes drain, and he was saddened by all this, but he did not despair. He travelled to the end of peril. Like the enemy or the king's men before them, he was drawn to the harbor city and its flourishing trees. The city was already poor then, already wasting, and my father's father knew that soon the trees would die. He had seen trees die before and he knew the conditions for their death. He stayed in the end of peril for many years. He studied the trees, and the soil and the air in which they grew. He married my father's mother, who was an heiress to forested land. She died before the trees did, and he brought her dead body, along with many living seeds, back to his own country across the ocean. He buried his wife in the ground, and above her, he built the dome.

He built the dome far from the megacities that sprawled over the coasts or drained the great lakes. My father's father irrigated and purified water from wells deep underground, he treated the toxic soil, reclaimed the land. As a young man, my father, who remained at the end of peril, had vowed never to live in the dome, in the false city his father had built. My father believed the city had killed his mother. He could not see it as anything but her tomb. But when I was born, my mother and my father believed the dome would be a safer home for me than the harbor city. They agreed to let my father's father transplant me there. I was his first human subject. The first citizen of the domed city.

When it was confirmed that the dome did not poison my infant body, my mother and father followed. Then, the other inhabitants my father's father had selected with an algorithm he took to his grave. My father's father was buried beside his wife under the dome. My father inherited a house on the city's edge and wrote books he never finished. My mother educated me. We lived together, in a house on a shady street, with verdant lawns and perfumed gardens, and for many years we were a family.

I DO NOT KNOW WHO cut down the trees at the back of the house. The construction men, I assume, though I never see anyone behind that chain link fence. The lot is always empty. It was abandoned long ago.

I think of the men on the street with their food carts and their thin arms and their gaunt faces and at night I see these same men working in the empty lot at the back of the house, cutting down the trees that no longer grow.

The men move quietly for their numbers. I do not hear them breathe. Their axes swing through the absent trees and come around and swing through their absent bodies and swing through history and through time, and the moon expands on such nights to fill the sky. The moonlight turns all to stone, and the house is petrified. The house where I was born. The house of my mother's girlhood and my grandmother's jewelry and my grandfather's books and the history of this family, and the history of this country, and the afterlife of all its peoples. It is a mixed-up and crowded place where animals, hungry ghosts, demons, hells, and human beings all live together.

In the lot, the men swing their axes through the trees and through themselves. I take my axe to the moon.

My father had a gift for storytelling.

When I was very young, before he got ill, my father would tell stories to put me to sleep. He made up legends of kings and wars and magic. His mother and his father were not of the same people and my father often told the story of their love.

Later, after my mother left, my father told me the truth: his father had married for land and his mother for passage. My father's mother, she wanted to leave the city where she was born. The city where my father was born and where I was born. My father's mother, she died in this harbor city. She never made it to the dome. My father's father killed her.

And my father was his father's son. He would have killed my mother if she hadn't left him. He would have killed me too.

There is a girl in the mirror who haunts me. She follows me around the house.

I see her in the windows overlooking the courtyard, I see

her in the glass of the chandelier, I see her on the mantel in the sitting room, locked in a gilded frame.

The girl is my mother and the girl from the domed city and my dead grandmother and the young woman the baby might one day become.

I sleep in a different room every night to escape her. I lie in various beds throughout the house, the baby asleep on my body, and I think of my days in the other city and how long ago it seems that I lived there with my mother and father and watched the leaves fall from my window. I think of the girl who had been my closest friend. I could never say to her what I meant. Thoughts aligned in my head into infinite vectors but would not escape from my mouth. When I spoke I was seized by a demon. Like my mother always said, I was possessed.

I speak to no one here but the baby. My grandfather sleeps. My mother decomposes before her mirror.

When you were born, my mother said, I prayed for a boy.

My mother, she did not want a rival. She possessed a singular beauty. She drove all men to madness.

I was born a girl but my mother's prayers came true. Now that I have reached manhood, my mother is driving me mad.

The enemy followed the river until it surfaced and gained strength and swelled over the banks in heavy rains and carved out the earth and pushed the opposite shore far against the horizon. They followed the river until it flowed into the delta and they could smell the salt of the sea and the rice milk and blood of the king's people.

The enemy drank rice milk and blood. They advanced down the river and the king's people retreated to the end of peril. The end of enmity. The end of strife. In the language of the harbor city, the two syllables of the city's name foretell its fate. Peril. Gone.

The king's people fled to the coast, the ones who survived the first raids, they fled to this natural harbor carved by the river. They settled between the two bodies of water, fishing along the coast, or tending the fields by the riverbanks where the ground was rich in minerals. The enemy encamped on the northern bank of the river and for many years waged a siege there against the king's men. Villages sprung up along the banks on either side and the river was set on fire.

The king had a daughter by a fisherwoman who lived on the southern bank of the river. Out of love for his daughter, the king built a tower with bricks molded from the red clay of the riverbank. He built the tower high to keep his daughter safe.

In the red tower, the king's daughter passed her girlhood. Every day she looked down upon the burning river. Every day she watched men die, pierced by flaming arrows, burned alive, or drowned.

The girl could not sleep in the domed city. She said the city was too quiet at night and too dark. The city was dead. The girl was afraid to sleep. She was not allowed to spend the night at my house, in the house where I lived with my mother and father. Neither my mother nor the girl's grandmother would allow it.

On new moon nights, or nights of a lunar eclipse, the girl would shine a flashlight through my window. The dome sky displayed the moon phases recorded in the old almanac and I could always predict when the girl would come. My mother did not lock our doors and the girl would walk right through the front door, up the stairs, down the hall past my parents' rooms, and into mine. She would climb into my bed and wrap her arms around me. Only then could she fall asleep. I did not know then that doors could be locked. A shut door was enough to keep me out. I kept my door ajar for the girl.

I SIT AT THE MANY windows of the house with the baby in my lap and make observations of the city. I try to be objective, but it has been many years since I last wrote a report for my mother and I have forgotten how to think like a scientist. Today the sky is light grey, almost white, though the undersides of the clouds are brown. Children in the street are straddling the trunks of street lamps that fell in the last storm. A dog is crushed under one and the other animals fight over its living flesh. An old woman naps nearby on her mat.

I have not left the house for many days because the baby has not yet recovered from its cough. I regret having taken it with me on my walks through the city when we first arrived a moon ago. I was afraid to leave the baby in the care of my mother, my mother who does not remember how she treated me as a child.

I am sorry, I say to the baby.

The baby puts its mouth to the glass of the window. The baby is watching. Even if the trees grow back in this city, thick and sweet at the back of the house, and the river turns blue and the fish silver and gold in the water, the baby has seen what it has seen. I am glad for this. I am not afraid to look at the dead, the sick, or the sleeping; the baby neither.

My mother used to hit me for chewing with my mouth open or sitting with my knees apart. She did not want to be reminded of the permeability of the body, of my body, which had invaded and opened hers. My mother wanted to close me up, to seal my mouth, eyes, ears, nose, anus and vagina so I was sanitized, so she could bear to look at me. My mother did not hit hard, but I always cried. She made my father watch, which is what I could not stand.

When I got older, I slept with men in the domed city to spite my mother. The men I slept with were married and older. They were happy to be with a young girl like myself. That is what they said to me. They did not mind that I was not as slender as my mother. They had never met my mother. They said they liked the girth of my thighs.

Afterwards, I always felt a searing hatred towards these men. They lay there on the bed in their own sweat, their flesh rubbed raw and damp.

I wanted to tell my mother.

Hit them, I wanted to say to her. Hit them for what they did, and I will watch.

At night, when the baby is fed and briefly asleep, I lie on the soft carpet of the nursery and listen to the howls of pack dogs, the night traffic sweeping by on a distant highway. If I listen closely enough, I can hear the ocean.

I think in the morning I will leave the baby in the care of my mother, and ride a bus to the city center. I have not seen much of the city. I would like to visit its markets and walk its crowded streets. I would like to see the ruins of the king's palace and the pagoda his wife built from her deathbed. I will forget the domed city with its neatness and exactitude. I will forget the girl and my father who I left there. I will leave this nursery, where I had lain helpless as a baby, and where my mother had lain before me. In the morning, I will settle into a room with more windows. I will look out these windows and I will see the ocean glittering against the horizon. In the sunlight, the water will look almost blue. I will walk to the back of the house, I think, and climb the chain link fence that separates my grandfather's land from the empty lot. The lot will no longer be empty then because I will be standing in it. I will run my hands over the trunks of the invisible trees that grow there and breathe in their stale, metallic air. I will emerge onto the street. There will be young men on motorcycles or mopeds waiting for me by the curb, and I will ride with them to the sea.

The chief's son could speak to animals, both living and dead. Many worlds were open to him. When he stood guard at night along the river bank, he saw the bodies of men, women, children and beasts gleaming as one globular mass beneath the surface of the water.

He watched the bodies separate and re-form, green bodies,

coated in ash, the blood drained from them into the mouth of a volcano. The sacred volcano where the dead slept. The traitorous volcano where they awoke. The chief's son watched the bodies borrow limbs from one another, amalgamate, then pull apart. The sky was black for many days after the eruption. Ice fell in smoldering shards. The bodies were always in motion, and still they always remained. Mud and ash from the blasted peak mixed with the melting snow and ran down the slope of the mountain.

To the chief's son, this seemed natural. Even the glaciers moved. The mud flowed and swept bodies away.

Sometimes when the girl shined her flashlight through my window, she would not climb into my bed, but stand at the threshold of my room and ask me to dress. She would stand there and watch me dress. I think she was looking for bruises on my body. The girl hated my mother. She wanted my mother to wake up and catch her there, in my room, or in my bed. She was not quiet when walking up the stairs. She stomped with all the strength of her small body. It occurs to me now that the girl might have come to my house even on nights when she did not shine the flashlight. She might have entered my mother's room or my father's room, and stood before their solitary beds. I do not know why she never killed my father while he slept. Why she never put him and me out of our joint misery. If she loved me. We never spoke of love, the girl and I. To speak of it was to ask for a sacrifice. I knew love was taught in school instead of algebra. Love of country. The girl spoke of standing still for half an hour, the exactitude of rituals surrounding the flag, the songs and postures she had to learn. She spoke of school and her mother with the same contempt.

She led me through the woods with her voice and the gleam of the flashlight. We walked all night through the trees surrounding our street, surrounding the city. We never once got lost. I had read in a book of a maze forest where trees moved to entrap those who ventured inside. The trees in the domed city also seemed to move, but not to entrap. They moved to show the way back. The trees formed a membrane that always guided us towards the city. And that is why we spent all of our time there, in the woods, to feel the soft net of trees catch us over and over again, the warmth of the city enveloping us, even as we walked its edge.

MY GRANDFATHER IS THE LAST doctor in this city, so I take the baby to him in the study. The baby coughs and my grandfather removes his spectacles, furrows his brows. Looking at my grandfather I cannot believe that my grandmother died in his care. I do not know how she died. Giving birth to my mother, I think, for I cannot imagine my mother with a mother, especially a mother as graceful as my mother's mother would have been, a classical musician, a rival, kneeling with the harp in her lap.

The baby has not been drinking much milk. I boil the tap water and sift the milk powder and still the milk makes the baby sick. The baby regurgitates what little it drinks in a thin, greenish paste. I think of my invalid father. All the years I cared for him, I waited for him to die, I prayed that he would die, and now my prayers are coming true, not for my father, but for the baby. I do not want the baby to die. The baby must not die. I say this to my grandfather though he does not speak the language of the domed city. Let it die not, please, I say in the language of this city. I can speak of death fluently in the language of this harbor city. It is the language we spoke around my father's bed.

The baby looks so small in my grandfather's hands. I worry that the baby's constitution is not strong enough for this city. The baby was born in the other, domed city, and though I also lived there for most of my life, I was born here, in the end of peril, and my life line runs straight. I will die far from the place where I was born. I will not die here.

When I die, my mother said, I will be reborn in your womb.

I shook my head. I was afraid for anything to grow inside of me.

I carried you in my womb, my mother said. You won't do that for me?

I imagined my mother shrivelling into a baby and crawling inside my body. I shook my head again.

Let me in, she said, nuzzling her head against my belly. I laughed because her hair tickled my skin.

Then she sat up and took my hands. I would hate to be a baby again, my mother said. I will live to be a hundred.

I wear my mother's old clothes when I leave the house. I find them folded in trunks in all the rooms covered with cloth. Only my grandmother's things are hoarded in my mother's room. I am walking to the pharmacist, an old friend of my grandfather's, to retrieve the medicine the baby requires. I have left the baby in my grandfather's study because I am afraid to expose it to the city air. I cannot take any risks with the baby's health now.

I left the baby and my grandfather both sleeping in the study. I will not be gone long.

My grandfather has written out a list for the pharmacist. I cannot read his handwriting but I can feel the list's importance. The weight of the paper in my hand. I learned the script of this city's language through my mother's old textbooks, and I can only read the round, printed font of those books. I write in that same font. My penmanship was my mother's pride.

In my mother's clothes, I walk to the railroad and cross it. I keep my eyes on my feet so I do not step in dog shit or puddles of acid rainwater. I am wearing the clothes my mother wore after her pregnancy, after I was born and regretted. My mother's married clothes, her mourning clothes. It is a miracle they are not riddled by moths.

There are tire tracks pressed into the mud beside the railroad, from food carts, I think, or motorcycles. The street is too narrow for cars. I have never been to the pharmacist before, but my grandfather says all I have to do is follow the railroad. He says I cannot get lost. My mother does not know I am wearing her clothes. Her somber blouse and heavy skirt. She has not asked after the baby for some time now. I step over or around the shit in the street, and it looks rather human to me. I never owned a dog, and I do not know what dog shit looks like. Sometimes there are maggots crawling in it. In the trunks in my grandfather's house, I also found the clothes my mother must have worn when she was my age, her school clothes, her two-piece sets and gowns. I cannot fit into them. She was a slender beauty, my mother. Shards of glass are stuck in the mud, and I have to avoid stepping on them as well. I am wearing sandals, also my mother's, and the leather is worn thin, poor protection in this street. Ants march over my uncovered feet, fat and red, and the spiders who eat them are fatter still. As long as I can remember, my mother has been thinner than me. She did not even carry me when I was a child. She said I was too heavy. My father used to carry me on his back or shoulders, but then he got sick, and he could not carry me either. The ground is stained red with betel nut. Betel nut is rare now: the nut palm trees are gone, and the betel vines are gone. Nothing grows any longer in this harbor city. If I look up now, I will see the old men on rain buckets staring at me. I drop my head lower and hide behind my falling hair. My mother had long, thick hair, straight as a knife, that fell to her hips. That hair does not grow from my head. I have too much of the enemy's blood in me, my mother always said. Our hair is wild.

The girl in the red tower was brought food and drink twice a day. Palm leaf manuscripts were delivered every waxing moon. The girl was well versed in the three baskets of scripture, the monastic rules and discipline; the discourses, teachings and poetry; psychology and metaphysics. She studied concepts of kingship, royal duties and powers, the rules of court etiquette. The king's other children were princes and princesses and the girl had never seen them before. When the enemy sacked the king's palace, which lay north of the city, the girl heard that the king had sent the royal family away to a safe place. A cave inside a mountain or an island far off the coast. A place safer than a high tower overlooking the river.

The king's daughter did not mind. She liked her tower. She liked to be close to the king's men. The girl felt too alone. Her mother was a fisherwoman who lived on the southern bank of the river and because the girl was a king's daughter, her mother was below her. Though the girl was not ashamed, the fisherwoman did not come to see her. Because the king was ashamed, he did not come to see her either.

When I left my father in the domed city, I killed him. He was an invalid; he could not live without me. Most of the people in the domed city thought I was his wife. They could not tell me apart from my mother. It was as if they had their eyes gouged out. To them, we all looked the same. My mother. My father. Myself. We were one people. One person.

When my father's father came to the end of peril to conquer it, to conquer my father's mother and her inheritance of land, he thought himself the first conqueror of the city, the first great man, for his height, his body hair, the raw pink color of his skin, his ghost eyes, and his red privates. The meaning of the city's name was lost upon him. The end of peril became the beginning, the mouth of the river from which my father's father and men like him forced themselves into the country, glutting the river and choking the people on their death ships. There was a war for the end of peril and for the country, and though it took place two generations ago, it is the same war that raged outside the domed city, the same war that is still raging now, against those who live outside the dome, though there is no dome left. It is a war against disorder and against life.

When I was a young girl, my mother taught me the laws of science. It was meant to complement my study of religion.

Both science and the religion of the king's people, my mother's people, rested on the universal law of cause and effect. My mother said that because of this law, the universe tended toward disorder. It sprawled and scattered. If it didn't, she said, all the planets and galaxies would stack up neatly, fitting together like folded sweaters in a drawer, and there would be no room for life. I imagined the earth crammed between Venus and Mars and the sun too and I looked out my window at the tree-lined street we lived on, the trees perfectly spaced, and the beautiful green yards separating each house from the other. I did not know then how much space life required. How much separation, how much loneliness.

THE PHARMACIST SENT ME BACK with a box of vials, creams, powders, and dried herbs, all of which she prepared before me on the lacquered counter. The box was made of real wood, fragrant, like the trees in the domed city. The pharmacist had bone white hair and skin dusted with age spots. She consulted my grandfather's list as she worked, but did not speak to me. I watched her withered hands as I waited.

I think one day my hands will age like hers. My hands will grow beautiful. The baby will grow strong. The baby is sleeping against my shoulder now. I have given it its medicine. I sit in the baby's nursery, my old nursery and my mother's, and rub the baby's back with mint and clove oil. The smell reminds me of my mother. When I was a baby did the domed city make me sick? Did I feel dizzy from the surfeit of oxygen there, as the enemy did, descending the foothills?

Sitting in the nursery with the baby in my arms, it is as if the baby is my mother, or myself, and it makes me feel lonely.

◆ ◆ ◆

In the other city, in the house where I lived with my mother and father, I was also very much alone and I often thought of the story my father had told me of a princess in a tower who was shut up there during a war. Because I was young and my mother had trained me to have a literal, scientific mind, I imagined the princess' tower at the very edge of a battlefield. But my father said, no, it was a battle by sea, so I imagined her tower built at the edge of a cliff and because I had never seen the sea before, I asked my father what it looked like. He said it was like the sky but bigger and darker, and always moving and he promised me one day he would take me to see the sea. I wanted to ask him what the sky looked like as well but I knew it was a forbidden question in the domed city, a question that would upset my father. Besides, my father said the battleships did not meet at sea, but upriver, and so I imagined the princess' tower on the banks of a large river, though I had never seen a river either, and at night, after my father left my bedroom and turned off the lights and years after that, when he never returned to my bedroom again, when he never got out of his own bed, I would look out my window, at the woods behind our house and imagine a great river and a great war.

Before the king fled to the end of peril, he buried all his wealth. Gold and precious jewels, fine tapestries, white elephants. He sacrificed his royal attendants, his concubines, his most trusted servants. In death, they were bound to guard the king's treasure.

There was no key that would unlock the king's vault. It was sealed by blood and could only be opened by blood. Blood spilled at the foot of each palace tower, and blood spilled at the foot of the throne. Because it was bad luck to spill royal blood upon the earth, the king had his wives and children buried alive.

Even the enemy knew of the curse of royal blood. How it could not be spilled upon the earth. In the enemy's religion, there were also such sanctions regarding the type of blood that could and could not be spilled. The blood of innocents, the blood of heroes. Both of those dead were martyred. The green dead, the un-ripened dead. They had to be appeased with offerings of food and whiskey. But the royal dead could not be appeased, except through seven generations of strife and instability. In the religion my mother taught me, the religion of the king's people, there are prayers that offer protection from fires, floods, black magic, weapons, contagious diseases, wild animals, thieves, robbers, and kings.

The king did not bury his daughter by a fisherwoman because she was not a princess. She was only his bastard daughter, a love child, and the king believed he loved her. He believed he had come to a haven. In the end of peril, the king believed, his treasure would be safe.

I could never say to the girl what I meant. Lying beside her in my bed at night, our feet lightly touching beneath the covers, I would listen as she spoke, as her words spun a soft net, a lid over our bodies. The girl's words, the roof, the dome. These were the layers of the other city.

The girl spoke of the woods and how she would find a way through them one day. The woods were a labyrinth, the girl said, and like any labyrinth, there was a way out. The girl wanted to tear down the trees. She wanted to tear down the black domed sky, and the pink sky beyond, which we had never seen. She wanted to tear them down to bring them close to her, to cover her budding breasts, to suck on in her sleep. The corners of the sky wet with her saliva. The girl wanted her mother to come home.

Still, she never spoke of her mother. The girl would turn to me in bed, her hair smelling of flowers, and tell me about her father. He lived far away, the girl said, in another city, a real one. Not made-up like ours, she said, not pre-planned and walled-in, and domed-over. A city with noise and lights and a pink, electric sky, always bright.

I was my father's young wife in the domed city. In this city, though I wear my mother's old clothes, no one mistakes me for my mother. I am an invader here. They know it by the girth of my thighs: the men playing chess on the sidewalk, squatting on their haunches, the schoolgirls with their faces painted by the grounded bark of extinct, medicinal trees; the tea shop keepers, stout and drowsy, in the shade of their verandas. All of them know it. And the animals too.

The only birds I see are already dead, caught by starving house cats or urchins gangs. The street dogs want to devour me. The insects. My body is milk white and fattened. I was fed by the wealth of the domed city, its green woods and added vitamins. My skin is smooth; my bones are strong. I have all my teeth and they line up straight in my mouth. I am a big girl. Many people had to die so that I could live. My mother, my father, my mother's mother, my father's mother and father, all the people of this city, the king's men, the farmers, the fishermen, the king's daughter in her tower. Their blood fertilizes the earth and the trees will grow back in the city, greener and more fragrant than before.

MY MOTHER'S WEDDING PICTURE IS hung up in the sitting room of the house. It is a large photograph, almost life-sized. It rests over the mantle. I do not know how long it has been there. I cannot imagine my grandfather hanging anything and my grandmother has always been dead.

In the photograph, my mother has flowers in her hair, a bough of jasmines pinned on one side. Her hair is combed and coiled and draped over her shoulders. It looks as if she is wearing a wig. She sits at the vanity, my mother, and you can only see her profile. The long forehead, the small nose, her slight underbite. Not her best angle, but the eye is drawn to her reflection in the oval mirror. She looks straight into the mirror, and straight out of the frame.

She is radiant, glowing like an apparition, for the beauty of the dead is always eternal and transcendent, while the living decompose.

MY MOTHER DOES NOT LEAVE her bedroom now, the room where she slept as a girl. The rooms in my grandfather's house have locks on them and my mother has shut and locked hers. At first, I left food outside her door, plain rice and dried nuts, the same offering I had made to the family altar every morning in the domed city. I thought of my mother as a saint. Not a disciple of the awakened one, but a green martyr who had made her way into the religion of the king's people, a spirit who had lived in the trees until she found a place on the perfumed altar. In the woods, descendants of the enemy would leave whisky or cigarettes for their green dead. On the altar of the awakened one, only water and plain rice was allowed, nuts and peeled fruit.

And just as my offerings to the family altar remained untouched in the other city, so does my mother's food. Every evening, I find the tray exactly where I left it beside her locked door. The nuts are soggy, the rice crusted, and the glass of water clouded with dust. There is not much rice stored in the stone pantry and the altar in my grandfather's house is dry and bare.

After days of throwing away my mother's food at the back of the house, watching the animals emerge from the ground to devour it, I could not stand to feel the eyes of street children on my back, the pinprick mouths of hungry ghosts on my skin. I stopped bringing food to my mother. I thought, I have killed my father in the domed city and now I am killing my mother in this one. It was the first precept, to refrain from killing any beings. It was the first duty of a child to feed and provide ceaselessly for one's parents. As part of my education I had learned the poem on the five duties of a child. I never learned the duties of a parent. My mother only said she fulfilled them.

In the other city, I had no future. I was not allowed to think of the future because the future only existed after my father's death and it invited much negative karma to ever want one's parent to die. One's parent who gave one life. But I did not ask for life, so I never understood why I was indebted forever to two people who gave me a gift I did not ask for. I suppose all gifts are unasked for. There was no future for me in the domed city; there was only duty and death. I had felt that I would die before my father did, that he would live forever and in my stead, another wife would appear, my own daughter, and in this way, my father would prolong his life. Is the baby my daughter? I wonder, as I look upon its sleeping face. Is it my son? Will it resent me for this gift I am giving it now, this life?

I am a mother now, I say to the baby, and my chest grows heavy. I am a mother without ever having been a wife, a lover. I was not a lover to the married men I slept with in the domed city. I was little more than a whore to them. But I had loved the girl, though we did not speak of love. Perhaps that was enough.

A love story was told to the children of the enemy and the children of the king's people. They are one people now, the children. The grandchildren and the great-grandchildren. The war and the war again and the wars that followed making one people where before there had been many.

In the story, the enemy's prince and a princess of the kingdom fall in love. The prince is a brave warrior. The princess is beautiful. There is a burning river that separates the lovers. One day, the prince catches sight of the princess in her tower and he jumps into the river. He tries to swim across the river and he drowns.

In another story, the prince is saved by a crocodile who carries him safely to the other shore. The princess catches sight of him emerging from the crocodile's mouth and she jumps from her tower. The tower is built too high and the fall breaks her neck.

In the last story, the prince rides in the mouth of a crocodile every night to meet the princess and every dawn he crosses back in the same way to his father's camp. Then one night, a battle breaks out on the river. The crocodile and the prince are caught between the warring ships. To escape the flaming cannonballs, the crocodile dives deep underwater until the fighting is over. When he emerges on the other shore, it is nearly dawn and the princess runs down from her tower. The crocodile collapses on the river bank. The princess pries open its jaws, and the prince's body drops lifeless into her arms.

The princess goes mad and jumps into the burning river. It does not end the war.

I told the girl the stories my father told me. I changed the details and made up what I could not remember, and in my mind, the enemy and the people of the domed city were one people. They were combined in the body of my father. My father was the son of an enemy chieftess and the son of an invader. The waves of invaders breaking upon the end of peril, each act of violence precipitating another. Because my father was descended from two waves of invaders and my mother was one of the few left with pure native blood, my body was war. In the domed city, my body was the spoils of war and in the harbor city, my body is the shame of war. I am a child of violence. But the stories are love stories. The princess and the prince. My father's father and my father's mother. Can there be love in a time of war? The loudspeakers in the domed city killed love, love between two people, even two children, between me and the girl.

They teach us lies, the girl said to me once. She meant at the school. We were sitting up in a tree in the woods. The girl was a better climber than me and on a higher branch. When I looked up I could not see her face. Her face was blocked from me by the trunk of the tree.

They say the war will end soon, the girl said. That my mother is a hero. They say the city will open and I will see her again.

The girl's voice was neutral as she spoke. It was the same voice that came from the loudspeakers in the city center. All of us who lived in the domed city knew how to imitate that voice.

I did not believe what the girl said just as I did not believe the loudspeakers. There was no door to the city. There was no key. The city could not be opened and still be itself.

Your mother is dead, I said to the girl.

Her body is bloated with water, the girl said.

This was how we showed our love to each other.

After some time, I climbed down the tree and began to gather my clothes from the bushes.

Are you coming down? I called out to the girl.

Yes, she said, her voice far away.

A wind blew through the trees, the artificial wind from the vents, and leaves floated down, brown and yellow.

THERE IS A STORM IN this city. I thought there had been storms before, but I know now this is the first one of the season. The animals have gone wild because there is nowhere for them to hide. The trunks of street lamps are not hollow like the trunks of trees. The ground is mud or slabs of concrete. The animals howl and throw their bodies against fences and brick walls. They beat their bodies until they fall down bloody. The baby cries because it is a small animal. My grandfather says the rain carries disease. It singes fur and feathers and skin. The street dogs are balding in patches and the children too. My grandfather says the rain blinds the young and poisons breast milk. My grandfather has retired to his study now. He will be safe there.

I have unlocked the doors on the ground floor for those who might seek shelter from the storm. My mother's room remains locked. I leave a bowl of rice porridge by her door. The baby's nursery faces the sea so the windows rattle the loudest there. There were no storms in the domed city, but there was the breach, and I am prepared to protect the baby. I find a small room in the middle of the house. It is almost a closet. A servant's room, I think, in the days when my grandfather could afford help. The room is on the second story so it will not flood, and if the roof flies off, there will still be the attic above us.

The walls of the house tremble. They feel so thin. The wind screams like a hungry ghost. Like all of its grief is pushed through a pinhole mouth. I think of my father in his bedroom, in the domed city, the trees puncturing the walls. For the first time, I am glad there are no trees in this city. In panic, the baby has latched onto my breast and I let it. I think of the girl in the other city, her hand in mine, the mud wet in our hair. I think of the girl walking into the woods, the baby in her arms. Or the girl standing still and the woods moving towards her. The baby has lately sprouted teeth and I feel it gnawing on my skin. I hear human screams coming through the walls. My mother awoken from her death, I think, or the street children come in through the ground floor. The doors swing madly now, slamming open and shut. The children, the wet dogs, the young girls with their long poles, the fish washed up from the river, the water rats, the birds, the spiders, the ants, all huddled together on the ground floor, under the gaze of my mother's wedding picture, under the protection of her undying beauty. The baby bites into my breast and blood gushes from the wound. The baby drinks thirstily. I think I hear my mother call out for me.

The storm lasts for many days or only a few hours. It is difficult to tell inside the closet of a room where I hide with the baby. The closet has no windows and no light. My breast stings where the baby bit me. My mother's blouse is wet with the baby's saliva and my blood. I hold the baby against my shoulder now so it will not bite me again. Because the baby cannot drink my blood, it cries. Because my body cannot produce milk. The baby's crying is incessant. It does not tire. In the dark of the closet, the baby's crying and the wind are the only sounds, the only solidity. After hours or days, I can no longer feel the baby against my body. I cannot tell where my body ends and where the baby begins. I can only feel the sound of the baby's crying, the sound's sharp edge. The crying gnaws at me, at the dark which is me and the wind. The wind carries the voices of the city's animals and the city's children and the city's miraculous elderly. I can hear the houses and buildings groaning in the wind, the billboards and street lamps crashing, the railroad tracks flying off, and their iron nails scattering like seeds.

There was a dark room my mother locked me in when I deserved it. Time did not enter the room. I had no name in there and no body. It was so dark, I could not see my own hands, only a line of light at the bottom of the door. I watched that light though I had no eyes, though my eyes too had been erased.

I died in that room several times. It is crowded with my ghosts.

When the storm is over, my mother is gone. The hinge of her bedroom door is broken. When I enter her room, I have nowhere to step. The contents of my grandmother's trunks are strewn all over the floor, wet from the rain that leaked through the open window. Fine silks and cottons, hand dyed batiks, laces, beaded shawls, ivory combs, embroidered slippers, parasols, they spill from the trunks like the softest of entrails. I want to lie down in their luxury. I want to crumple.

The bed is unmade, and the curtains are drawn around the four posters. The oval mirror, which leans against the wall, is cracked. My mother has released herself, I think. I look out her open window at the flooded streets below. The water is thick and brown, shining like the skin of a soap bubble.

The bowl of rice porridge at my mother's door is empty.

IN THE DOMED CITY, THE body was divided into its component parts and each part studied for disease. At the hospital, the corridors were labeled with the names of these isolated body parts and their diseases. The corridors of the hospital were wide and carpeted and the ceilings low. To walk the length of the corridors was to review my knowledge of physiology and my mother allowed me to wander while she sat in the waiting room, telling beads and chanting silently so only her lips moved. My mother was pious as all vain, beautiful women are.

The hospital had a chandelier hanging at every rotunda where the corridors met, and at the center of the building was a glass courtyard. Patients stretched their limbs there and breathed double filtered air. The hospital was built just like the museum with its rounded roof. It was built just like the opera house with its curving stairs. All the buildings in the domed city were alike.

When I grew tired of the long corridors in the hospital, I would walk the rim of the balcony overlooking the glass courtyard. I would look down upon the sick gathered there and imagine they were bacteria growing in a petri dish, multiplying and multiplying, like the cells inside my father's body.

The baby is unwell again. Its recovery has been hampered by the storm. I think the baby has blood sickness from drinking my blood. Blood gives life and yet carries disease. I am afraid the baby has developed a taste for my poisoned blood milk because it will drink nothing else. I boil water from the stored jugs and seep the dried leaves I retrieved from the pharmacist. The baby will not drink its medicine. I pinch its little nose between my thumb and forefinger, I squeeze the sides of its small, pink mouth. I am afraid the baby will choke. I do not know what else to do. It coughs and coughs. What little milk or medicine I force down is spewed up in pale scraps.

Outside, the streets are still flooded from the storm. The ground floor of the house is still flooded. A wet dog is stranded on the sofa in the sitting room. I would like to help the dog, but my grandfather had said the rainwater eats away skin. Besides, the dogs in this city are vicious. No one will care for the baby if I am bitten by a stray dog. If I am infected and if I die. The dog is large and black except for bald patches on its flank where the fur has burned off. It is pink in those patches. The dog shivers from the cold. I think it will shiver off its life. When the dog lifts its head, its eyes are rolled back. I can only see the whites of its eyes.

◆ ◆ ◆

My lifeline cuts the palm in two, just as I cut myself from her, my mother said. A mother and a child were one body. I cut the umbilical cord with my sharpened enemy's teeth. The river cut open the city.

From my mother's old bedroom. I have a clear view of the sea. I could not see it before from the house but the storm has raised the sea over the dikes and levees. The delta is flooded. The paddies are inundated with salt. Families sleep on the roofs of their houses. The young girls I saw in the street with their wares on long poles now traverse the streets in makeshift canoes. Children float in refrigerators, paddling with their hands. I do not look closely at the children. I do not want to see how their fingers have been eaten away by the acid rainwater.

The baby will drink a little rice milk, but not its medicine and not its powdered milk. I rub the baby's small body with ointments. I bless its body. The tip of its head, the point between its eyes, the base of the throat, the center of the chest, the solar plexus, the stomach, the pelvis. I would show the baby to my grandfather again but my grandfather's senses are dulling. When I enter the study now he mistakes me for my mother. He calls me by her name. In the damp of his study my grandfather has wrapped himself in wool blankets. He has built a fort of books around his desk. It is his burial pyre. In this city the average man lives to be twenty-five years old. Because my grandfather is the last doctor he has lived thrice as long. Soon he will die. The dying cannot help one another.

◆ ◆ ◆

The chief's son knew of the witch in the red tower, the king's bastard daughter. It was bad luck to look upon her tower, the women of the camp said. Her face was a curse. A child had seen it, on the last full moon, and had died within three days. The child had collapsed in fits, bit off his tongue, and almost choked on it. He died of the blood-sickness that followed.

The chief's son saw the dead child's body in the river at night. Floating belly-up in the flaming water, the child gazed upon the red tower with his black, luminous eyes. The child's mouth gaping slightly open, black blood pooling at the corners. The girl never came to the window when the child was looking. When the chief's son was looking through the dead mirror of the child's black eyes.

The chief's son ran his tongue over the bottoms of his teeth, pressing against the sharpened canines. His teeth had been filed when he became a man. He bit down on his tongue until it bled.

I SIT AT MY MOTHER's vanity before the cracked oval mirror. When I was young my mother made me clean all the mirrors in the house because she believed it would make me beautiful. My mother pressed my teeth with a wedge of wood every night to straighten them. She pressed my forehead with the palms of her hands. She pinched my eyebrows to give them shape. She pulled my small ear and pressed the larger one against my head. I wanted to be beautiful so the pain would stop, but every day in the clean mirror I would see the same face. My wild face, the enemy's face. This face stares out at me now from my mother's oval mirror. I do not look at it. I am looking for my mother in the mirror, the girl inside the mirror who haunts me. I brush my hair with an ivory comb I found on the vanity. I have to remove my hair from its teeth after every few strokes. The comb was not made for hair like mine. It is engraved with elephants. I drop it. She has gone to die, my mother. If I follow her, I am afraid I will die too, and the baby. All I do is follow my mother. The lines on the palms of her hands are deep and mine are faint. My mother is strong and I am pulled into the stream of her life.

The velvet stool I sit upon is bloated with rain and the wet seeps into my clothes. The room smells of mildew. I have not bothered to put back my grandmother's things into the trunks where they belong. The night he left the palace for the holy life, the enlightened one awoke surrounded by the sleeping bodies of his court musicians and dancers. Their bejeweled limbs contorted in poses of death. My grandmother's finery is strewn on the floor like those gaudy corpses.

Where are you? I ask my mother's ghost in the mirror. She does not appear. I cannot remember what her face looks like. When I close my eyes to imagine it, I can only see the young woman in the wedding picture. The young woman who has no relation to me, a stranger. I do not think my mother was meant to grow old, to become a wife and mother, to dilute her pure blood with another's, a man's, a husband's. My mother should have died a bride, so all her life could have been, all her beauty, her intelligence, her grace. Where are you? my reflection in the mirror asks. I am sitting on my mother's velvet stool, at my mother's vanity, in the room that had belonged to my mother when she was a girl. I am haunting my mother, I realize. It is not the dead who haunt the living, but the other way around. We are the ones who remain, who linger, when the dead have long departed.

The ashes of the dead in this harbor city are scattered in the river, so that is where I will go to bury my mother. Though my mother's body is missing, I know she is dead. She died long before she disappeared. I will go to the river to perform the funeral rites for her. It is time I perform the rites for my father as well. I must release both of their spirits into the next life. It is one of the five duties of a child. I am my mother and father's only child. If I do not fulfill my duty, I will bring misfortune upon the baby and myself.

The river is also where the baby first fell ill. By returning there, perhaps I can release the illness that possessed the baby. The water of many rivers is said to heal. The renewal will bring many miracles, the people of this city say. I have heard them speak of the renewal with more fervor since the storm. They believe the storm is auspicious. They believe the ocean will carry the seeds of the flourishing trees back to this harbor.

The only miracle I want is for the baby to get well. I want the baby to live, and to live a long life. I want it to see this harbor city as my mother saw it when she was a girl, the woods thick and sweet at the back of the house. I want the baby to see the city as my grandparents saw it, and my great-grandparents before them, as the enemy saw it when they arrived on the northern bank of the river, and as the king's men saw it when they retreated here and named it the end of peril.

The enemy believed that inside the cocoon of the body lived a butterfly. The butterfly would emerge from the body while a person slept and fly through the three worlds. The world of the living, the world of the not-living, and the changing world.

The chief's son was taught as a child to protect his butterfly by tying a red string around his toe. This way it could not fly far from his body while he slept. The souls of children were capricious and sometimes forgot to return to their bodies. A soulless child did not live long. The empty body collapsed upon itself.

When the chief's son became a man, he bit off the red string with his sharpened teeth. His butterfly flew through the three worlds and thereafter all three worlds were visible to him.

The citizens of the domed city were chosen by an algorithm that my father's father invented. Some were the families of national heroes, like the girl and her grandmother. Others were the country's most talented scientists, partners in my father's father's research. Although the domed city was a closed system, self-sustaining, it still needed maintenance. The citizens too needed maintenance. We had doctors of every specialty, engineers, biologists, teachers. My mother and father might have been the only unproductive citizens of the domed city. We were the only family living there on account of blood. Even the girl's grandmother worked as a school teacher. The girl told me she had been a professor before they came to the dome. In the domed city, there was no university. Young people learned by apprenticeship. Because I was apprenticed to my mother I learned how to care for my father and how to be idle.

The girl did not want to be apprenticed to anyone. She did not want to become a productive citizen of the city. Sometimes the girl frightened me. I did not know the extent of her power, her will, what she would do or become. She was like a princess locked up in a tower. I was devoted to the girl because I knew I was below her. I was a coward. I feared her and I feared the war raging outside of the dome. Though there was no outside of the dome, though the city was everything I knew.

I told the girl the story of the princess of the kingdom, and she said the princess was a fool for giving up her life for a boy.

Not just any boy, I said, an enemy prince.

For betraying her father then, the girl said.

The girl did not believe what the loudspeakers preached about love for the fatherland, but she loved her own dead father, which amounted to the same thing.

I would not fall for some enemy prince, the girl said. I would disguise myself as a man and fight to defend my country. I would be a hero.

Although the girl hated her mother who was fighting in the war, she was her mother's daughter. A soldier, a warrior.

SMOKE ESCAPES FROM MY GRANDFATHER'S study and wafts through the hallways of the house. He is burning books. The ink burns neon green and gives off an acrid odor. A toxic odor, I think. Everything in this city is toxic. The books also smell of burnt flesh. Animal vellum. It makes me hungry. If I shut the door to my grandfather's study and trap him inside, he will die from the fumes. There are no windows in the study, no ventilation but the chimney. There is no wood to burn in the fireplace, so my grandfather has thrown in a chair, a costly antique. The chair is broken into pieces. The strength of the dying is incredible.

I knock on the open door of the study and announce myself.

Mother is gone, I say.

My grandfather is seated in his armchair, beneath layers of blankets, a pile of books at his feet. Even from where I stand at the doorsill, I can smell the thick, metallic smoke coming from the fireplace. I press the baby to my chest to shield it from the fumes.

I am going to the river to bury her, I say.

My grandfather lights a match and watches it burn. He does not drop the match even when the flame licks his fingers. He will burn down the study, I think. He will burn down the house.

I am taking the baby with me, I say.

My grandfather does not look up. He opens a book in his lap and lights another match.

In the domed city, no one noticed when my mother left. One day, I finished my lessons, and the next day my mother was gone. I was the new mother in her place. It was as if my girlhood had left instead of my mother, as if our family had lost a child.

The neighbors did not show any sympathy for me, our family's dead child. I had plucked flowers from their garden as a child and for that they called me a thief. They said I did not belong in the domed city. They told me to leave. My mother had never been able to protect me from the neighbors. She had not even been able to protect herself. My father was his father's son and only the blood in his veins protected us. I plucked the flowers in our neighbors' garden to make them bleed. I broke the necks of the smaller buds and ripped up the faces of the larger ones in bloom. I left them to rot on the ground.

I imagined what it would be like to do the same to my father, to pluck him from his bed, from his tubes and wires and plugs, and leave him to rot in the front yard, on our green lawn, which watered itself every day. My father's body wet from the sprinklers, distended, ready to burst. A lawn mower approaching, its blades slicing the soft grass. I bathed my father with a washcloth every day, administered his pills, took his vitals, turned his body, emptied his bedpan, fed him with a spoon, and this was how I imagined my father, sprawled on the overgrown grass, inches from the shuffling, wet blades.

I have emptied one of my grandmother's trunks to use as a canoe. The streets have drained enough for me to wade through them in a pair of fishing boots I found in the house, but a canoe will be the best way to transport the baby and our provisions. The baby is bundled in a warm blanket and outfitted with a filter mask. I place my grandmother's parasol at one end of the trunk to protect the baby from the sun. There is no shade in this city and I do not want the baby to be sun-poisoned. The baby's skin is milk white. It was born in the domed city under a blue sky.

I drag the trunk down the stairs to the ground floor and I am relieved the black dog I saw in the sitting room is gone. Though I never owned a dog, I know they like to die alone. The fine upholstery of the sofas is sodden and shredded where stray animals have clawed at it in fear. The glass of the coffee table is broken, and the chandelier lies in a heap on the muddy rug. Only my mother's portrait hanging above the mantel is untouched by the storm. Inviolate. I put the baby down in the trunk and secure it there with my grandmother's silk, which I have knotted into rope. My grandmother's silk was spun from silkworms, but other caterpillars also spin silk cocoons and spiders spin silk webs. Silk feels soft and delicate, but is incredibly strong. I had read in a book that spider webs can catch even birds in flight. I pull the trunk from my rope of silk into the foyer and make for the door.

◆ ◆ ◆

When the king's daughter was too young to care for herself, there had been a woman who fed and washed her. The king's daughter could not remember this woman's face, only the softness of her body and how she smelled of earth and jasmine. This woman was not her mother. The girl's mother, the fisherwoman, had not been allowed to nurse her.

Both her mother and the woman were gone now and the king's daughter fed and washed herself. Twice a day food was brought to her tower. The village children who delivered the food did not dare to look upon the king's daughter's face. It was forbidden to look into the eyes of a princess, an offense punishable by death, and though the king's daughter was not a princess, but the daughter of a fisherwoman, still the children were afraid. Her blood could not be spilled upon the earth without cursing the land for seven generations.

In the days after my mother left the domed city, I thought often of the princess in my father's stories. Was she heartbroken too, I wondered, that her mother had left her? That her mother did not visit? Was she sad to be alone? I did not know whom the princess loved. The woman who had nursed her when she was young? Her father, the king? I did not know whom she was saving her love for.

Sitting by my father's bed all day, or lying in my mother's empty one, I could understand why the princess might have fallen in love with the first person who showed up at her tower, the first person she met in the woods, the first person who saw her naked, or only in a pair of white underpants. Even as a child, I feared that had we not lived in the domed city, had there been more children at the school, the girl would have never been my friend. We had nothing in common. She was nimble and strong and brave, and I was an oversized doll sitting still at my lessons. I did not understand the girl the same way I did not understand the princess. That is what I admired about both of them. They were so enigmatic, so womanly.

A woman should be absent of desires, my mother had said. She must never want a man.

Because I did not want any men, I believed I was a good woman. After my mother left me, I wanted no women either. I was absent of wants. I did not even want to leave the domed city as the girl did. I wondered if the princess wanted to leave her tower. Sometimes a prison becomes a home. The princess had been imprisoned by her father and I had been imprisoned by mine, but still, I could never be the princess. I was not beautiful or courageous. But it wasn't as simple as the girl was the princess and I was the prince, because the prince was brave too. I am neither the princess nor the prince. Sometimes I regret ever coming to this city. I should have died in the dome, stay locked in my tower so there would be no story to tell.

WHEN I EMERGE FROM THE house with the trunk and the baby, it is dawn. The sky is white. The lot at the back of the house is ravaged. The chain link fence has fallen over and the locked gate is broken and hanging open. Mud is caked upon every surface. The baby begins to cry as it floats away in the trunk, and I realize I have dropped the silk rope. I pick up the rope again and tie it around my wrist.

The construction in the lot looks like a building torn down instead of a building half-built. I can see the holes in the ground where the dead trees were exhumed. The concrete that covered the holes has cracked in the storm and pried off. The holes are filled with mud and rainwater. The rats drowned. The invisible trees are glutted with rain, to rot and die again. In this city, poor families burn their dead and scatter the ashes into the river. Now the river has flooded and heaved the dead back upon the earth. I make my way through the broken gate, pulling the baby behind me in the trunk. The streets are unrecognizable. Bent metal signs in the cracked windows of buildings indicate what purpose each space had once served: tea shop, tailor, bicycle repair. I think of the pharmacist and if she could help the baby now. If she is still alive. The food cart men are pedaling through the streets again, splashing muddy water as they pass. Women walk holding sandals in their hands, their skirts rolled up to the knees. In every yard, girls are rushing to and from the gate, emptying buckets of water into the street. It is futile work. The water from the street runs down the slope of the yards, and into the houses again.

The baby is asleep in the trunk, rocked by the pull of wading bodies and bicycle tires cleaving the water. The silk rope already cuts into the palm of my hand. The trunk is heavy. The idle days in my grandfather's house have weakened my body. The days of lying on sofas and soft beds. My body has softened, too, like the ground after rain. I can hardly remember what we endured in the wake of the breach. When we retreated to this city, the baby and I, to the end of peril. We came here for refuge, as the king's men before us, and like the king's men, we are now trapped with our backs to the sea. My mother was right. This city is no haven; I cannot rest here.

When he walked upon the red earth of the riverbank, the chief's son touched feet with the dead. The world of the dead mirrored the world of the living. Their sky was the black of dirt and their stars were glowing tapeworms. The chief's son felt the presence of the dead most strongly by the river. The dead, or the unborn, for in the world of the not-living, there was only one time.

The martyrs all dwelled in that world. Their grief was too heavy to bear across the changing world, where all was light and quick. The boy's mother was a martyr. Her blood had mixed with volcanic ash and turned green. Her blood had spilled into the mouth of the volcano. The people of the camp prayed to the boy's mother for protection. They built her small houses inside the trunks of trees and left gifts for her there.

The chief's son looked for his mother as well, not inside of spirit houses, but inside of the river. He looked for her face among the mass of bodies that glowed below the surface of the water. The bodies that ebbed and flowed, seemed to breathe. Their faces were always changing and always the same. Black fish eyes and parted lips, skin shedding in delicate strips. Many nights, the chief's son longed to join the dead and the unborn, to slip under the river's current and let the burning water envelop his body.

Once my mother left the other city and I took her place as my father's young wife, the girl hated me as she had hated my mother. The girl was in my mother's room sitting on my mother's bed, draped in my mother's clothes. I could not meet the girl in the woods anymore so she came to our house. My father could not be left alone. The girl loved to try on my mother's things, hats, scarves, perfumes. My mother had taken little with her when she left the domed city. She said where she was going, the clothes she wore here would brand her as a whore.

I did not like to watch the girl touch my mother's fine things. Her fingernails chewed down and dirty. The girl said she knew some men who could help us.

I said, you mean your boyfriends from the school?

The girl said no, these were older men, powerful, they could take us away from the city.

I had not told the girl about the document my mother had left me. How she said I could follow her when my father died. I was afraid the girl would kill my father, that telling her of the document would be the same as asking her to murder. The same as me murdering my father.

Are you jealous? the girl said.

I looked at the girl sprawled on the bed, my mother's dress gaping at the chest where her small breasts did not fill out the fabric.

Take that off, I said.

The girl did not move. We looked at one another. She slid the dress off and stood up from the bed. She was in a pair of white underwear, just like the first day I met her in the woods.

I'm leaving, the girl said.

Okay, I said.

BY THE TIME WE MAKE it to the railroad the sun is high overhead, and I begin to worry for the baby. The houses and buildings fall away and the old men who used to sit by the tracks are gone. Dead, I presume. I do not see their rain buckets. Their three-pronged stools. Their imitation betel nut. Gangs of wild dogs and children have gathered at the railroad to fight. It is difficult to tell one pack apart from the other. The dogs are bald and ruddy, and the children are coarse and hairy. I must find a way to cross the railroad and reach the river. I must perform my duty to my mother and father. I must burn their bodies and pray over the pyre and release their butterflies into the changing world. A butterfly trapped too long inside a dead body cannot fly far. The children are growling, and the dogs scream. I think of my father's body punctured by the trees. My father's body, the walls of our house, and the dome sky of the other city. The three breaches from which I escaped.

The children and dogs are wrestling now. The children are armed with scrap metal and shards of glass. The dogs with their claws and teeth. I have nothing to protect the baby and our provisions, the grains of rice, jugs of water. The children and the dogs are hungry. They are devouring each other as they kill.

I turn back from the railroad before the dogs and the children see us, and push the trunk toward a pile of driftwood washed up by the storm. I shut the baby inside the trunk. It will be safe there, inside the mouth of a crocodile. I cover the trunk with some wood and junk metal I find lying around. I want to make sure the dogs and the children will not find us. When I think the trunk is hidden well enough, I open it again and climb inside. I pull the lid shut. We will wait here until the railroad is safe to cross. In the trunk there is no room to move or breathe. We have arrived at the lowest level of hell, I think, a cube buried deep inside the earth. I am afraid the baby cannot breathe. I hold my breath and listen for its soft exhalations. The baby squirms against my body. Its little kicks fill me with hope. The baby is alive.

I have not spoken to the baby for some time, and I am sorry. I had been distracted by the storm, I say to the baby, my mother's disappearance, the preparations for the journey. I had been occupied with rationing the pantry supply in my grandfather's house, dividing the rice into three portions: one for myself and the baby, one for my grandfather, and one for the women who came to the house every evening, their open hands thrust through windows broken by the storm, hands missing nails or fingers, discolored and diseased. Some of the women carried babies in their arms. The babies were probably corpses or sacks of stone, but still I gave food to the women, jewelry, silverware, whatever I thought they could sell. The first practice of the holy path is generosity, I say to the baby, sacrifice.

In the dark of the trunk, the howling of the street dogs and street children slowly dissipates. I pray the dogs and children will be satiated by each other's flesh. I pray they will not smell us. I brought no weapons on this journey, and I have nothing to protect the baby and our provisions. In the domed city, there were no weapons, no locks on the doors, no screens on the windows. The city was the end of peril, enmity, and strife. In the domed city, there were no wild animals or people I needed protection from. I did not learn how to fight. My mother only taught me how to run, and my father only taught me how to die.

I teach the baby now how to give. I tell the baby of the generosity of the awakened one. How life after life he had given away his inheritance, his eyes, ears, nose, and tongue, his arms and legs. Many times he had given his life. He had thrown his body into a deep ravine so a starving tigress could feed on it. So her body would produce milk for her young. So she would not eat her young.

Don't worry, I say to the baby, I will never eat you.

I laugh. The baby does not laugh. I roar like a tigress, and the baby begins to cry.

One night, the king's daughter received a letter from her father, the king. The letter was brought to her tower by a young woman from the village. Maybe the woman was her sister, the girl thought, or her father's newest concubine. The king's daughter was filled with love and hate. She wished her mother, the fisherwoman, had been sent instead.

Up in her tower, the king's daughter looked upon the burning river and thought of a story she had read, of a monkey king who made his body a bridge so the smaller animals could cross a river to safety. There was a great conflagration in the forest, or else an enemy clan approaching. The king's daughter could not remember. She only felt the great pain of the monkey king, his strength, how he endured those panicked feet trampling the length of his body. How he loved his people. How much he sacrificed. The king's daughter had wept for the monkey king when he died, when his back broke and he fell limp into the river. She had wept for her father.

The king's daughter broke the seal of her letter and held it up to the light of the candle burning by her window. A ship had been built, the king's letter said. It would take her away to the queen and her children. The royal haven. She was to leave on the night of the new moon.

You are my daughter, the king wrote, and you will be protected as a princess.

The king's daughter rolled up the letter, and looked out her window again. She had never been addressed as a princess before. She did not know how to feel. She looked out the window and the moonlight fell across the burning river like a bridge.

In the days after my mother left, I felt a heaviness settle into my body, my stomach, solar plexus, arms, shoulders. Even my head felt heavy. There was no space left inside my body that was not filled with this heaviness. My chest hurt. It was hard to breathe. All foods tasted acidic and I lost the desire to eat, to fill my heavy body even more. I did not think: I miss my mother, I miss the girl. I did not miss my father as he used to be before his illness. I could not remember what my father had been like.

I missed hunger, sleep, and desire. I felt like an old woman, like my father's wife, the wife of a dying man. I tried to think of the girl who had been my closest friend, but she no longer seemed real. I could not believe that I had ever had a friend, that I had ever had a mother. I became mother. I began to remember the past through my mother's eyes. While taking my siesta, I would dream of my wild daughter in the woods. Then I even forgot I had a daughter. I became mother without antecedent. I no longer knew what mother meant. Mother tongue. Mother country. Motherland. A land of mothers where every tree was once a mother and now every tree has been chopped down. The chief's son had no mother; I had a mother; and yet it amounted to the same thing. There could only be one mother in a story and because mine was possibly still alive, the girl's mother had to be possibly dead. The chief's son's mother had to be definitely dead, and the king's daughter, though she had a mother, was not allowed one. Since there could only be one mother in a story, I killed my mother when I became mother. When I became my father's wife in the domed city, and took her place.

I CANNOT MOVE INSIDE MY grandmother's trunk, and a young man opens the lid and asks to come inside, and he has the look of a man who has come from far away, a place farther than the domed city, a place I cannot go, and though the man does not speak I know he is asking to lie down inside the trunk, to lie inside my body, and I want to hold the man to my body, but I cannot move, and he does not move, and the stillness between us hardens over his face like a mirror. He has the face inside the mirror, the girl's face that haunts me, my wild face, the face of the enemy, and I am lifted from the trunk by this face, I am looking inside the trunk, I am standing inside the man's body, inside the glass of the mirror, and I know he is a man because his teeth are filed sharp, like the crooked teeth inside my mouth that my mother could not straighten. I bite down gently on his tongue, I taste my blood, I am careful not to spill it upon the earth, I am careful not to spit and curse the earth. I look inside the trunk and the baby is so small it will fit in the palm of my hand, a round, furry seed. I will plant the baby inside the earth, and the renewal will come to this harbor city. The trees will grow again, and the baby will be born from the earth, born a second time in the place of my birth, where my parents were born, and my grandparents before them, and only the man who has my face, who lives inside the mirror, will know where I have planted the seed of our baby.

THE BABY'S CRYING BRINGS MY body back inside the trunk, where it is cold and wet. I lie in the damp and listen for the howling of the dog children. I shush the baby and listen harder. I am afraid I will suffocate the baby, pressing my hand over its face. I can hear nothing but the baby's whimpers. I release my hand. The baby has stopped crying. Still I cannot hear the dogs nor the children. I push at the trunk's lid. It is heavy. I open it with some difficulty. The driftwood falls away like bones, splashing as it hits the pools of water on the ground. I step out of the trunk and retrieve the baby. The sun is still up. It floats thick and white in the brown sky.

We must find the river before dark, I say to the baby.

I remember there were stilt houses along the bank, and we can seek shelter in one tonight. Some of the houses must have withstood the storm. I knot the silk rope of the trunk around my waist and hold the baby in my arms. We wade towards the railroad. As we near the tracks, I smell the blood before I see the bodies. The children and the dogs. Dead, they are even more difficult to tell apart. Hair or fur matted with blood, pink entrails, quivering and wet. The baby looks at the corpses with something like hunger and it frightens me. This harbor city is a curse. For once, I do not want the baby to look. I hold the baby's face to my chest. I protect it from this city.

We cross the railroad, and the ground slopes down on the other side. I can just make out the stilt houses by the river, but the water is so high the stilts are covered. The houses float like dry leaves.

There is a path through the rice paddies, a strip of elevated land. I had followed it to the river in the days before the flood, in that month of rain and idleness. It had led me to the bluff. I think I can make out the dunes of the bluff now, but the sun is so bright they might be a mirage. The sun turns the water gold. It would be almost beautiful if it weren't for the smell. Manure and formaldehyde. It makes my eyes sting.

I wrap the baby to my chest the way I have seen it done by other women in this harbor city. The women who used to come to my grandfather's house to beg. I wrap the baby because I will need my hands. I tie my grandmother's trunk to the stump of a streetlamp and turn back to gather rocks from the railroad. I stay clear of the battlefield where the bodies of the dog children lie. Insects are already swarming there. Flies the size of the baby's fist.

When I have filled the folds of my skirt with enough rocks I return to the trunk. I wade out as far as I can into the flooded paddies and throw my rocks. Where the water swallows the rocks, I turn away. I was careful to find rocks of equal size and weight. My education was accelerated in the domed city, and I know how to conduct an experiment. I know how to control variables. When I have only three rocks left, I find it, the strip of elevated land. The rock splashes loudly there. The water level is shallow. I pull the trunk behind me and push towards the path.

The moon grew fuller and fuller in the sky each night. It pushed the darkness down behind the mountains or deep into the sea. It edged into the corners of the sky and pressed upon the horizon. It waxed and waxed until it filled the sky, until the sky shone white, resplendent, and none could sleep beneath it.

The girl in her red brick tower could not sleep. She lay awake under the bright sky and read her palm leaf books and plaited her long, black hair. Holding her hair between her fingers one night, the girl ceased her plaiting. She climbed out the window of her tower and up onto the sloping roof. Balanced there, she held up the sharp blade of her hair, and struck it against the low, smooth sky. A sliver of moon fell down in her lap. She struck again, and again.

Sleepless children ran through the village, trying to catch the moonflakes in their small hands. The light caught in their hair. Their eyes were wet. For many nights, the king's daughter carved up the moon, the black knife of her hair the only darkness in the sky.

When her work was done, the darkness rose from behind the mountains, and from under the sea, and covered the night again. All in the kingdom fell asleep and only the king's daughter was left awake. It was the night of the new moon.

◆ ◆ ◆

In the domed city, the seasons were so mild that time did not seem to touch me there. The trees turned yellow and brown and their dry leaves fell to the earth; they stood naked against the sky; they sprouted green buds and fragrant, white flowers; and inside the walls of my father's bedroom, these changes had no meaning. My father's body was ruined.

There was nothing more they could do for my father at the hospital, but I still brought him there as my mother and I had always done. Though I was my father's new wife, or his old wife, for the doctors mistook me for my mother, I could not sit in the waiting room as she had, telling beads and chanting under her breath. I did not know what to pray for. Instead, I walked the corridors as I had when I was a girl, as if my mother had given me permission to, as if she would be waiting for me when I returned to my father's ward. The diamond patterns on the carpet were familiar and the low ceilings comforting. I walked slowly and without purpose, and the corridors led me to the girl.

She was sitting in a waiting room identical to all the others in the hospital. Her face was wan and strange, but it was her, the girl who had been my closest and only friend. I stood for a while in the corridor thinking she would look up and see me. She did not. I had stopped next to a window and the sunlight warmed my skin. I remembered then it was summer. A year had passed. I walked closer to the girl and she looked up and saw me. I could never say to the girl what I meant. I did not say anything to her then. I sat down.

I thought I would see you here one day, the girl said.

I looked at her face and tried to decipher what had changed.

I wanted to tell you, she said.

A year had passed since my mother left, since I last saw the girl.

I can feel it kicking now, the girl said. She smiled in a way I had not seen her smile before.

Do you want to feel it? she asked.

Yes, I said, and the girl took my hand and placed it on the swell of her body.

ON THE NIGHT OF THE new moon, two of the king's men came to fetch the king's daughter from her tower. The girl was ready for them. She had packed all her possessions in a wooden trunk: her palm-leaf books, her fine clothes spun with gold, her pearls, her ivory comb, all gifts from her father the king. She had packed a brick she pried from the wall so she would not forget the red clay of the riverbank where she was born.

The girl blew out the candle by her window, and in the dark, the king's men led her down the winding steps of her tower. The men did not carry lanterns and no light shone through the slit windows of the tower. The king's daughter felt as if she were falling into a wide abyss, as if the ground were crumbling beneath her feet. They emerged into the night and in the light of the low fire still burning on the river, the girl looked upon the faces of the two men. They seemed weary, their skin scarred. Like the children in the village, the men did not meet her eyes.

The three of them walked long into the darkness, following the river, but far enough from the shore so the enemy would not see them. They walked through fields and dense woods and always the king's daughter looked for the flickering light of the fire burning upon the river. The river was a battlefield glutted with death and yet it made the king's daughter feel safe. It was all she had known. They walked and walked and the two men did not speak to each other nor to the girl until she forgot they were there with her and she walked as if blind, as if descending her tower again, the trees falling before her hands, the ground falling before her feet, and the light of the river quivering, coaxing her closer.

I think I see drowned bodies below the surface of the water. Bodies bloated with acid rain, green, purple and black. The skin is cratered where fish have begun to feed, the appendages fraying. I see green stalks of rice stream from split heads and gaping mouths. A milky film grown over the eyes. Long plaits of hair swimming between my feet.

Maybe they are water snakes, I say to the baby. I do not want it to be afraid. The animals in this city have multiplied since the storm. There are many birds flying overhead.

Look at the birds, I say to the baby.

I hitch the baby onto my shoulders so it can see. The birds are noisy and the baby is quiet. I look up and I can see the bloody beaks of the birds. Their metallic claws. I bring the baby back to my chest. Its face is shriveled and grey.

We are going to the river to make you better, I say to the baby.

The river has flooded to cleanse this city. It will cleanse the baby too. The baby caught its illness from the river, and we will return its illness to the river. The people in the streets believe the renewal will come. The people in the golden temples. The people in the stilt houses. We pass two farmers in a canoe, a man and a woman. They are bent over the water harvesting what rice they can. They do not look up at me and the baby. I do not call out to them. I look at the man and the woman, in their matching conical hats, and for a moment I want to give the baby to them. The children in this city either grow strong or they die. The baby must make a choice.

I do not remember the walk to the river being so long, and it grows longer with each step I take. The baby grows heavier in my arms. I think of my grandfather for the first time since I began this journey. It was only this morning that I left my grandfather's house, but I feel as if it has been many years of war. How long has it been since I left my father's house? The baby is a measure of time. I bounce the baby in my arms to feel its weight. My arms are tired. I had wrapped the baby to my chest for some time until my shoulders began to hurt. Now I hold the baby in my arms again. It seems to have grown smaller since I left the domed city, but heavier, like a stone. I think of my grandfather in his study, the fireplace burning green. I see him burning my mother's wedding picture, the life-sized portrait which hangs over the mantel. My mother's spirit released from the gilded frame. Like a stone or a rock, the baby feels solid in my arms. I think of the rocks from the domed city, which I dug out with my hands. The rocks smooth and identical, shaped by my father's father, his machines, his scientific learning. It was my father's father who poisoned the trees in the domed city. Poisoned them not to die, but to grow hysterically, like the cells inside of his body and inside of my father's. My father's father is the architect

97

of the breach, the renewal, and even the storm that has wrecked this harbor city. My three inheritances. I do not know what I will leave behind for the baby

The witch girl in the tower did not sleep. Every night the chief's son stood watch by the river, he saw a light in her window. A light from candles made by the fat of his kinsmen. A second death by fire for those who had drowned in the burning river. The chief's son did not sleep either. The window of the bastard's tower shone like a false moon in the sky. A red moon, the chief's son thought, the mouth of a volcano.

Then, one night, the girl's window went dark.

It was the night of the new moon and there was no other light in the sky. The stars were veiled behind thick clouds; the fire burned low on the river. The king's shore lay in darkness. The chief's son looked inside the river, and saw only his own reflection on the water, his wild hair, his protruding brow, the one ear larger than the other. He had his mother's face, the chief's son had been told. The face of a martyr, a face built to endure pain. In the reflection of the water, the chief's son caught movement at the base of the girl's tower. He looked up and saw it again. Dark shapes in the trees. A rustling where no wind blew. The king's daughter running away.

If he captured the girl, the chief's son thought, he could ransom her for the harbor city. He could end the war. He waved his torch to the other guards along the river, then extinguished it in the sand of the riverbank. The king's bastard could not know that she was followed. If she moved in darkness, so would he.

THE LINES ON THE BABY'S palms are still forming. I place the baby's little fists in my mouth as I walk, and hum a blessing. May the baby's life line curve back, may it die only in the place where it was born. When the baby is old, I think, hundreds of years from now, for the baby will live so long, the domed city will be habitable again. The baby can return there and marvel at the trees. The trees that grew so tall they punctured the sky.

I do not know who your father is, I say to the baby, but all mothers and fathers are the same.

I am going to the river to bury my mother and father. Nobody died in the domed city so I have never been to a funeral, but my mother taught me the religious customs of the king's people and the customs of the enemy. We are one people now. My mother prepared me for my father's death. I have been preparing for it for most of my life, and I know what I must do. Sewn to my shirt are two silver coins that will pay the toll for my mother and father to cross into death. I found the money in a beaded purse inside my mother's room. To appease the spirits who live in the earth and in the water, I have prepared an offering of yellow rice. There were spirits who lived in the trees as well, but they cannot be appeased now. They roam the city and possess the bodies of beautiful young women until the women sicken and die. I am not beautiful so I do not have to be afraid.

The funeral for my mother should have begun as soon as she died and ended after seven days. It has been seven days now since my mother disappeared in the storm. Seven days since the storm ended. My mother should have been buried on the third day after her death, but I do not know when she died. I do not know for how long the storm raged and on what day of the storm she jumped or fell out her bedroom window. I do not know if she survived the flooded street, if she is still alive.

After the day at the hospital I did not see the girl again. That is, when I saw her again, she was no longer the girl, but a mother, and because I only had one mother, all mothers were the same to me. The doctors told me to take my father home and keep him there. They told me not to come back to the hospital.

He does not have long to live, the doctors said.

Still, my father did not die. He lived through the summer and the trees grew in the woods, and I took my father's darkening hands in mine and searched for his lifelines. My father's fingers were black because blood no longer flowed into them. I could not make out the lines on this palms. The days grew shorter, the marvelous sun waned in the sky, the projection of constellations tilted in the dome at night, and still the trees did not shed their leaves and my father did not die. The trees were budding new leaves, larger than before, leaves that opened like hands, and flowers that bloomed white and fragrant.

The chief's son set off upriver. He went alone, as a scout, in case the king's daughter was laying a trap for his father's men. He followed the rustling of leaves in the woods on the opposite shore. The chief's son had discarded his torch and only the burning river guided him through the darkness. The dead left footprints for him to follow.

As the chief's son moved through the darkness, he thought he heard dogs barking on the opposite shore. The barks sounded almost human, like the screams of children. The sound frightened him. It seemed to reach him from far away, farther than the king's shore, from a place he could not go.

The flooded fields stretch in all directions around me. The sun sinks into the water. I walk faster, afraid night will fall before we reach the river. My arms and legs tremble from the physical strain. The baby is bound tightly to my chest.

The bluff in the distance pulls closer and I can see wild grass dancing over the sand. Grass flickering like fire. The sun is a red eye that holds me fixed in its stare. I walk faster and faster but my body does not move. It is the horizon that moves towards me. The rushing waters of the river, the stilt houses rising along the bluff. The houses are made of wood and my body is made of stone. I feel my body sinking into the mud, sinking back in time. The sea birds spiral overhead, and trace out words in a language I cannot read. The birds are singing strange songs. My body feels so heavy. I see lights flickering on the water. Canoes. Farmers. Fishermen and women. The drowned. There is the sound of children's voices in the fields. I hold onto the baby and force my legs to push through the mud.

A village appears along the riverbank. I can see it clearly now. Stilt houses with thatched roofs and canoes docked to the posts. They shimmer like a mirage. There are villagers and their beasts returning from the fields, small children at their games, fishermen and women hauling in their nets, glistening in the red sunlight.

Do you want to eat fish tonight? I ask the baby.

I imagine these fish will have silver scales and white meat and bones so soft the baby could chew them with its newly sprouted teeth. I feel hungry for the first time since I began this journey. I walk faster. The water splashes at my feet. The baby squirms in my arms like a slippery fish. If I drop the baby in the water it will swim away.

As the village nears, I smell fried fish and rice milk and burning wood. I hear the villagers' voices, their laughter, and the wind moving through leaves. There are trees in the village. Trees thick and fragrant. Invisible, like the ones at the back of my grandfather's house. I run my hand through the trunks of the trees, through the heavy air. The sounds of the village hold for a moment, taut like the strings of a harp, and then fall away. The fires burn down. The villagers sublimate. The village is empty. We have reached the river, the baby and I. The sun slips under the water and all goes dark.

THE KING'S DAUGHTER EMERGED FROM the trees onto a small cliff and saw that it was nearly light. No fire burned on the river this far from the king's city and the waters were calm and still. There was no ship.

The girl looked up at the faces of the king's men and at last, they returned her gaze. She looked into the eyes of men who killed.

Where is the ship? the girl said. The men did not answer. One took a step forward. The girl stood still and held her body erect.

My father said a ship had been built, the girl said.

The man lunged and took hold of her body. She fought him.

Where is the ship that was promised to me? she screamed. The man's body was made of stone. He closed his hand over her mouth. The other man dragged the girl's trunk to the edge of the cliff and emptied its contents into the river. The pages of her books scattered on the water like dried leaves. The three baskets of scripture. Poetry, psychology and metaphysics. The man did not throw the trunk into the river. He dragged it back to the girl and laid it on the ground before her.

◆ ◆ ◆

The day of the breach, I was in my mother's room, lying on my mother's bed, trying on my mother's clothes and thinking of the girl. My father was dying in the next room. My mother was dying in the end of peril.

I heard the sound of wings beating against glass, and in my mother's white silk dress, I got up from the bed and went to the window. The sound was coming from the leaves. Green leaves budding and growing and pushing against the glass. They looked like cards shuffling in a deck. I went downstairs and opened the front door and saw that the trees were growing, the trees lining the street and the trees in the backyards. The woods at the end of the street were swaying, rising like a green wave about to crash. I ran up the stairs again. I did not shut the front door. I did not change out of my mother's dress. I retrieved the document my mother had left me from under my bed and ran to fetch my father from his room. I meant to unplug him from the wall and carry him on my shoulders down from the mountains of ice.

When I entered my father's room, and I saw him lying there, in his bed, the tubes and wires sprouting everywhere from his body, I lost my strength. The trees had already punctured through the walls, and there were flowers blooming on the branches that had entered the room, flowers perfumed and white, their green tendrils creeping toward my father's bed, curling around his machines and drips. My father's eyes were closed, strained. His chest moved erratically up and down. I did not know if he was asleep, or just in too much pain to open his eyes. I left him there, on his deathbed. I did not say goodbye. I ran down the stairs and went to look for the girl.

♦♦♦

In the darkness, we listen to the sounds of the river, the baby and I. I am listening for the voices of my mother and father. The silver coins I brought for their burial burn in the palm of my hand. The metal feels cold and blue. I am to place the coins under the tongues of the dead. I am to clean and dress their bodies. In the darkness, the water sounds loud and close. There was no moving water in the domed city and the sound is unfamiliar to me. It is the sound of the renewal, I think. The sound of burgeoning trees. The sound of change. When I walked to the river in the days before the storm, the sounds of traffic and the fisherwomen's chatter obscured the voice of the river. Now I can hear it clearly.

My mother and father are not here. I have no bodies to burn or bury. I retrieve my offering of yellow rice anyway and spill some of it over the earth, some over the water. I place the silver coins beneath adjacent rocks on the riverbank. I recall all the prayers my mother taught me and recite what verses I find most appropriate for a funeral. Impermanence. The body as foam. I perform the water libation with a little of what is left in the precious jugs I brought from my grandfather's house. I do not know if I have saved enough water for the journey back.

When I finish my recitations and the water libation, the baby is asleep in the trunk. I do not know if I performed the rites properly. If my mother and father are released. I do not even know if they are dead. In the darkness, I cannot believe it. I feel as if it is the baby and I who are dead.

SHE BIT DOWN ON THE hand of the man who had held her to his chest. She bit until she tasted blood. When the hand released her, she screamed for her father. Her father who had said she would be protected. The king's men pushed the girl into the trunk and she clutched the lip of the trunk so they would not shut the lid on her finger. The king's daughter knew they would not spill her blood upon the earth, her blood that would curse the earth. One man held her down while another pried her fingers loose. The lid was shut. Nails driven into the wood. All was dark. There was no space to move or breathe inside the trunk. She threw her whole body against the wood. She felt the trunk moving. Her hands and her feet were free and she felt along the edges of the trunk for a loose nail or a splinter. All was smooth wood. She ran her hands over the trunk again in panic. She thought to bite off her tongue. Then she found it, by her knee, the brick. The red brick from the tower her father had built out of love for her. The brick molded from the red clay of the riverbank where she was born. Miraculously, it had been lodged in the corner of the trunk, and had not fallen into the river. The king's daughter nudged the brick up with her legs. The trunk was moving and she had little time. She felt the brick against her thigh, scraping her skin. She was nearly at the edge of the cliff now. Sand was seeping into the trunk. She scraped the edges of the brick with her fingertips. The river bank. The trunk tilting. At last the brick was in her hands. She felt for its sharpest edge. She brought it to her throat. May my blood curse this city for seven generations, she thought. The trunk fell into the river.

I ran to the end of our street, to the woods where the girl and I used to play together. I did not know where else to look for her. The neighbors were rushing in the opposite direction towards the city. They did not pay attention to me. The sirens and loudspeakers filled the air. The words evacuation and emergency and designated. Then I heard only static. I ran into the glutted woods, into the rising trees, and looked everywhere for the girl. The rocks my father's father had planted were loosening from the earth and moved beneath my feet.

I ran down the familiar paths the girl and I had walked at night. The paths twisting and meandering, sometimes ending abruptly, sometimes opening like secrets. I ran until I was lost, for the first time, in the woods. And at last, I saw her. She was standing on a pile of rocks in a clearing, holding the baby in her arms.

Because I could never say to the girl what I meant, I said only her name. I held up the document in my hand.

My father is dead, I said, I can take you to the end of peril, the end of strife, the end of enmity.

I climbed up the rocks to the girl. I wrapped my arms around her. I wanted to weep. The baby was pressed between our bodies and it was warm and soft and because I loved the girl it was as if I had birthed the baby myself. The girl held the baby in her arms and I held her and with the baby between us. We did not need to speak of love. The trees were thickening around us, their leaves unfurling, blocking out the light.

I'm sorry, the girl said.

She pushed me away from her body. She handed me the baby.

Please, she said, go.

When I did not move, she pushed me again. I stumbled down the pile of rocks, slid through a gap in the trees. I clutched the baby tightly to my chest. I looked up at the girl and the trees were closing around her. I could not see her face. I made my way through the tightening tunnel of trunks and leaves. I held the baby to my body, and because I had played in the woods all my life, because I had climbed the trees and marked them with my name and the girl's, the trees gave life to me and the baby. They delivered us from the dome. We emerged under a pink open sky, with the woods trailing behind us, like an after birth.

The chief's son hid behind the tall grass and watched as the two men thrust the girl into a wooden box. The chief's son had thought the two men were the girl's guards, but he saw now that they were her abductors. The two men were dressed in the king's colors, so they had to be traitors. The chief's son knew that tyrannical kings were often betrayed; he knew his father was not the king's only enemy. The chief's son had to retrieve the box and rescue the girl from her assassins. The king was said to be fond of his bastard daughter; he would not watch from the opposite shore as the chief cut off the girl's hands and feet, as he cut off her head. The two men were pushing the box to the edge of the cliff now. The chief's son knew what they meant to do. He ran downstream to where the river narrowed and driftwood created an eddy along the shore. He slid down the mud of the river bank and hid behind the trees there.

The trunk landed flat and floated downriver. The chief' son waded out into the cold water. He could not see the two men on the opposite shore. There were sea birds flying overhead. The trunk was nearing and the chief's son prepared to swim out and block it with his body. The sky was paling. The chief's son heard the dogs barking again. Maybe it was the king's daughter crying from inside the box. He swam out to meet the trunk. The current of the river was strong and the chief's son had to fight it with all the strength in his body. He wrestled the box as he would a crocodile. He could not breathe. The sharp water stung his eyes and throat. At last the lid of the box opened and broke off and the chief's son was pushed down into the muck of the river. The bodies of the green dead swarmed him and held down his limbs. When he surfaced again, the water was still. The box floated gently downriver and a red cloud trailed behind it, red blooming over the water like lotus flowers. The chief's son smelled blood. The red bloom was blood gushing from the box. The blood flowed as if from a wound, as if the river itself had been cut open.

The chief's son had drifted closer to the king's shore now. There was a woman standing on the bluff. At first the chief's son thought it was the king's daughter, that she had escaped the box and swam ashore, but the woman on the bluff was holding a small child in her arms. Her clothes and her long hair were dry. The chief's shook the water from his eyes and swam closer to the king's shore. He took another look and was sure of it now. The woman had his face. The same face he saw in the water every night, his wild face. The same protruding brow, the same sharp teeth, the same mismatched ears. The woman was his mother, the chief's son thought.

He forgot about the king's bastard daughter floating down-river in her box. Her royal blood cursing the water and the land. The chief's son spit the blood from his mouth and plunged into the river again, making for the king's shore.

The river rises before me like a wall. On the other side, I can see my mother. Her long straight hair, her rare beauty, a singular beauty that has no rivals, that would have chopped off my head had I been beautiful, my hands, my tongue, that would have gouged out my eyes. The water rises like the trees had risen in the other city. The renewal has finally come. The water in this city is the dome of the other city. It will enclose this city, this haven, this end. The baby is heavy in my arms. I wonder if it will be beautiful. I wish I had given it a name. The girl's face ap-pears before my eyes inside the wall of water. She is drowning in the water. Her blood turns the water red. I hold the baby in my arms. The girl holds out her hands. She bleeds profusely from her neck. My closest friend. She reaches out her hands for the baby, but I do not move. The baby was freely given to me. I will not give her the baby. The girl is drowning but she is not dead. She will not die until she has the baby. But the baby must live. I place it down on the ground by the river bank. I lay it down in the mud. I am sorry, I say to the baby. The baby's breaths are shallow but it is alive. If I cover the baby with the earth, it will grow. I do not. I walk into the water, the mirrored wall. I walk into the river where the girl is waiting for me, where my mother is waiting, and where my father has drowned himself. This city is not my haven. In the domed city, my lifeline ends. The girl will take me there.

When the boy makes it to the opposite shore, the woman who had been standing on the bluff is gone. Only a wooden box lies in the sand, identical to the one he had wrestled in the river. Next to the box is a heap of wet cloth. The boy picks it up and sees that it is the child the woman had held in her arms. The little thing opens its black eyes and coughs. The sun has risen and the blood on the boy's skin turns to water as it dries. The boy does not turn back to the river. He holds the child in his arms and walks into the thickening trees.

Acknowledgments

I AM DEEPLY GRATEFUL TO Valerie Sayers for her care and guidance as I was writing the first draft of this book; to Joyelle McSweeney, Azareen Van Der Vliet Oloomi, and Steve Tomasula for being my first readers; to my fiction cohort at the University of Notre Dame for their constructive and encouraging feedback; to Laird Hunt, for his generous support through the process of finding a home for this book; to the kind people at Noemi, especially Suzi Garcia and Emily Alex for their thoughtful edits; to Dennis for reading a draft of this book and affirming that it wasn't terrible; and to my friends and family, Mommy, Daddy, AKT, and Maswe for always being my biggest fans.